They Walk
Among Us

Donna J.A. Olson

Darkest Temptations

They Walk Among Us is a work of fiction. The characters and scenes are created from the author's imagination or used fictitiously. Any resemblance to real life people or places is purely coincidental. In no way is any story or character used in this book true. It is all created from the author's imagination.

This book is the recipient of the 2019 Canada Book Award.

Also by Donna J.A. Olson

Behind The Realms Series
Two Parts Love
The Peace Of The Sea
Tears Of A Valkyrie
The Queen Of Thorns

Other Titles
The Unhappily Ever Afters
The Darkest Fairytale

A Treat For The Reader

As a treat to you ad my lovely readers I decided to
take the creepiness of this book to the next level. I
created tarot cards based solely around this story for
you. I know that it is not a full deck, nor are they
traditional tarot cards, but I thought they were creepy
and cool none the less. They can be found between
the pages.
Enjoy!

History

So I thought I would give you all a bit of a history lesson. Dunvegan Provincial Park and historic site is the site of one of Alberta's earliest fur trade posts and missionary centers. It is located on the banks of the Peace River just off of Highway 2, 90km North of Grande Prairie and 26km South of Fairview. In 1805, Archibald Norman Macleod established the trading post naming it Fort Dunvegan after his home in Scotland. The buildings that are still remaining from that time are the Factor's house and the St. Charles Rectory and Church. In 1960, the famous Dunvegan Bridge was built.

Around the area, you are prone to hear ghost stories about Dunvegan. There is nothing that says any of these ghosts are real or if they are things that could be easily explained away. Being from the area I grew up listening to these different ghost stories, none of them are concrete and there is nothing that says that the 'ghosts' that exist were actually living people.

I have decided to take just a couple of those stories and give them life and a story as though they had existed and lived real lives. Before that life was harshly taken away. I just gave life to fiction. So read and Enjoy!

From Beautiful To Deadly

Chapter One

'The boundaries which divide Life from Death are at best shadowy and vague. Who shall say where the one ends, and where the other begins?' -Edgar Allan Poe

You believe that you have nothing to fear.
That we are simply apparitions of the night.
But we are not the ones you should fear,
instead, look to those who are out of sight.
If we truly wished you harm, you would already be dead.
No breath would come from your lungs,
As you lay there in your bed.
And yet you stand there wagging your tongues,
Taunting and jeering as you do.
Thinking that you are safe from harm,
Is the surety that you are completely screwed.
Do not worry for we are not the striking arm,
We will simply watch,
As Your torment will be Unseen but sure.
You will be but another notch,

Soon forgotten and seen as a lighted blur.
You will join us soon,
As an apparition of the night.
Living an afterlife of gloom,
For losing life's fight.
Maybe you should look closer before its too late,
We are not the ones you should fear,
We are simply the bait,
Drawing you near.
The story we tell,
Will be about just four.
The hateful way in how we all fell,
From simple heartache to an all-out war.
True there are many,
Who walk over this land.
From child, warrior, and ladies,
All struck down by someone's hand.
But ours are the stories most well known,
Even if all spoken is not true.
We wish to give voice to our mournful moan,
And tell all that we have gone through.
We were never wept for or mourned,
Our names became a simple whisper in the winds.
Forced to listen to our names and existence scorned,
Lives cut too short is what we pined.
Many lurk here,
Deep in these depths.

But there are four that are near,
And wish to finally recall our deaths.
We will tell all just this one time,
Of our existence in these rolling hills.
Existences cut short from bad luck to all-out war
crimes,
Stories that will make your body run cold with chills.
I am not speaking of a simple death,
Nor do I have a proper burial.
Everything was stolen in a single breath,
So these words will be my memorial.
These words will be spoken once,
And then never again to the living.
We will fade back to our durance,
But do not mistake for we will still be existing.
We will return to being the beings in the night,
That simple flash,
That you see but believe to be just a light,
In a way, we are the embers beneath the ashes.
Difficult to see at the time,
But bright and existing none the less.
So we exist here between the Heather and wild
thyme,
Wishing for someone to here us profess,
The horrors that happened many years ago,
Coating the river in red,
Tumbling the hills into the shadows,

And leaving our secrets to the dead.
The hills, the river, and the lake,
Are where our stories began.
Forces of earth and treacherous snakes,
Are what brought down the hard-hitting hand.
We are the forgotten,
Who haunt you in the night.
The ones who were left rotting,
But with a story left to write.
We are all just figments,
With a voice that needs to be heard.
We are like you but different,
Our lives just a little more blurred.
You may wonder where we live,
Or at least where we rest our souls.
It is a place that has outlived,
Us with our many life goals.
It has been there for centuries, for all its many years,
Changing as they pass.
Watching as life and earth disappears,
Creating a new great mass.
But with the changes,
There is much that must stay the same.
We have our faces,
But what is sought after is our name.
We are the ghosts of Dunvegan Park,
In the high North of the Alberta beauty.

Coming out mostly in the dark,
But also in the day but doing oh so mutely.
We are not known far and wide,
Like many of our kind are.
But unlike them, we do not hide,
From those who find us bizarre.
These are our stories,
From our life into our death.
While they hold fear and worries,
They hold the moments of our last breaths.
They are all filled with sadness,
From time's harsh hands striking us down in our prime.
So we apologize if the darkness,
Overtakes us with time.
The memories are dark,
And not always kind.
From Nun to Clerk,
To a misty Lady who is hard to find.
You may not know us now,
But soon you will.
You will be brought the truth that shall,
Make your blood run cold with a chill.
This will be a horror story,
The harsh strike of fate.
Are deaths torturous and gory,
And our existence now filled with hate.

That is all I will state,
For I will let the stories tell themselves.
Let them take you through the gate,
Into the past itself.

Judgement

The Woman On The Hill

Chapter Two

'Death is a delightful hiding place for weary men.' - *Herodotus*

I am the first to tell my tale,
Known as the Woman on the Hill.
I am not one to weep and wail,
But I have a story to tell still.
Look to the North hill,
That's where my spirit is found.
Brought about by winter's chill,
My existence is now eternally bound.
I am not a fancy lady,
Nor was I rich in life.
But my life was one that ended badly,
And not because I was simply a mother and wife.
I always did as I was told,
Until that single night.
The consequence cannot be a simple scold,
Because I lost life's fight.
My name is Abigail Porter,

I was a loving wife and mother.
But my life was cut shorter,
All because of the weather.
Roaring winds,
And blistering cold.
A flurry that blinds,
In a storm that came tenfold.
But if I am going to tell this tale,
Then I should do it right.
I will tell you of the trail,
I took that very night.
The winding twisting path,
But also what led to it.
How I suffered fate's wrath,
Passing away within the moonlit.
The story will begin,
When I still lived and breathed.
When I lived within my own skin,
Before my life was regretfully seized.
Before the night that changed my life,
And my very existence.
How a simple light,
Could hold such consequence.
Listen good and listen well,
For I walk among you still.
Because this is the place that I dwell,
And you just trespass against my will.

The Betrayal

Chapter Three

'What we have done for ourselves alone dies with us;
what we have done for others and the world remains
and is immortal.'
-Albert Pike

Love had no part in marriage,
At least that was what we were told.
We were to be ladies and never embarrass,
The husbands to which we were sold.
Money in exchange for children,
Was always how it had been.
To refuse made you a villain,
But to accept meant a bloody scene.
Doctors were hard to find,
When you lived in the middle of nowhere.
Which meant childbirth could only be defined,
A miracle but deadly affair.
I expected to no more than tolerate,
The man that was to be my husband.
But I could not help but fixate,

One this kind and loving man that could be trusted.
I was wed at a young age,
Just as many girls were.
But my marriage was not a cage,
That was of one thing I was sure.
His name was David,
And he was the love of my life.
Even though it was belated,
The love came and made me truly feel like a wife.
Just as my sisters' and brothers',
Our marriage was arranged.
But as time passed I found the wonders,
That never seemed to change.
David was all that was kind and gentle,
That I could not hold on to my fury at fate.
Since the match could not be accidental,
I decided to let go of my hate.
With my hate now gone,
My fear soon followed.
Leaving my joy to act on,
Leaving the rest shadowed.
As the joy blossomed and bloomed,
The love was next to come.
A love that made us feel consumed,
And made us joyous at what we had become.
My husband and I moved into a home,
Down in what is now known as Dunvegan Park.

It was something that was all our own,
And made me as happy as a lark.
Life was good,
We were happy as can be.
Feeling just as we knew that we should,
We wanted to make our two three.
"My beautiful wife, while I love you so
I wish for a son or daughter to spoil.
I wish to watch my child grow,"
David brought up as she watched her cooking stew
boil.
"I wish for a child to pamper and play,
But life is not so easy.
I am not sure if we will have our way,"
I replied feeling uneasy.
He stepped forward and took my hands in his,
And looked deep into my eyes.
I suddenly knew what is,
What he tried so hard to disguise.
"I know it will not be an easy trail,
That we choose to follow.
But if do it and we fail,
We will have no need to wallow.
"For we would have tried our best,
Finding that it is not our fate to have this child.
But if we are oh so blessed,
Our happiness will not be mild.

"It will be great and large,
And filled with love to the brim.
A beautiful merge,
Of a love that could never dim.
"So I ask you this,
I do not challenge or charge.
Will, we find our true bliss,
And make our family that large?"
Looking into his eyes so deep,
I did not know what to say.
Did I really want to reap,
Such disappointment by saying nay?
But did I truly wish to say nay,
When I wanted a child too?
Could I push my fear away,
And do what I wanted to do?
Or would I constantly hold my anger,
At being sold as a prized cow.
Meant only to breed and pamper,
And to do only what my husband would allow.
Tears filled my eyes,
And clogged my throat uptight.
I could no longer disguise,
My dreams that burned so bright.
I wanted a child to hug,
I had a dream to be a mother.
I could no longer ignore the tug,

I decided to give in to my wonder.
The hate and anger needed to be let go,
So that I could finally be free.
A fairy tale was not something that I would know,
But this felt like something that was meant to be.
I let a smile claim my lips,
As I gazed up at my wonderful husband.
I knew that I could finally fix,
This and find our joy in abundance.
"My fears and worries still hold true,
But I choose to fight past that.
I would love a child too,
I do believe I am ready to give it a try at.
"I make no promises,
Hear me now.
I will be honest,
This is what I will allow.
"If we are blessed with a child so sweet,
We will be as happy as can be.
But if we are not so blessed to greet,
A baby we must agree,
"To not be mad and hateful and cruel,
To one another for the loss.
For us to not let our emotions rule,
But for it to be our job to bear the cross.
"I will do this now,
If it does not change what we have together.

We will make this vow,
That we will always be tethered forever.
"A loss will not change our love,
That we hold so dear.
We will never be some mourning dove,
And will always fight for our cheer.
"I love you most,
And I will love a child too.
We will always remain close,
No matter what we go through."
A grin lit up David's face,
As he hugged me close.
He was my true ace,
The man I didn't know but in the end, chose.
"You make me happier than anything,
To be so brave right now.
My sweetest wife you are amazing,
And I will always hold true to my vow."

The Bloody Sword

Chapter Four

'We can easily forgive a child who is afraid of the dark; the real tragedy of life is when men are afraid of the light.' -Plato

Worry and fear,
Struck like a tornado within.
But it did not take long for us to be in the clear,
And calm took over instead of the whirlwind.
I had nothing to fear,
For soon a baby came.
And we held him oh so dear,
And finally, we had so much joy to exclaim.
We called him little Joseph,
After David's father great.
We no longer felt so hopeless,
But joyous in our happy fate.
It may have taken years,
But this child was a miracle.
Blessed by the heavens and stars,
So perfect and adorable.

Our family had finally grown,
We were now a happy three.
If I had only known,
I would have had a child sooner with glee.
We watched our little one grow,
Until he was soon a toddler.
But I had not seen the woe,
Or the edge on which I tottered.
The winters in Alberta,
Were harsh with a cold that bites.
We were too poor to afford thick parkas,
And the storms they blew so white.
The wind crashed against the shutters,
The storms howled loud in our ears.
While the flakes flew in beautiful, white clusters
The cold could freeze your tears.
The wind and cold chilled you to the bone,
But it was even worse for children.
Joseph had yet not grown,
Enough for the cold not to bother him.
A fever took him fast,
And it raged on like fire.
We could not wait until the storm had passed,
Our circumstances were dire.
With a kiss goodbye,
David left.
To fight through the nasty, snowing sky,

And bring the doctor that was the best.
The storm grew worse,
And my fear grew still.
I wondered why fate would be so perverse,
To constantly test my will.
I wondered how it could be so brutal,
To first give life and then attempt to take it away.
Was everything in life so futile,
All I could do was pray.
"Please, God. Save my son."
I pleaded with a cry.
"I pray for the sun,
For you to clear away the terrible sky.
"For my husband to return to me,
Safe from all that might harm him.
I pray for my son to be free,
Of his fever oh so grim.
"They are my loves, my life, my everything
Do not take them away.
I cannot watch them suffering,
As I sit here crying nay.
"Oh please God, protect them,
Or take my life in turn.
They are the true gems,
While I am not but a fern.
"They are life and true goodness,
Leave them in this world.

Drain me until I am bloodless,
And toss me into the underworld."
Hours passed,
But the storm raged on.
Leaving nothing but a vast,
White storm refusing to be withdrawn.
Joseph's fever refused to break,
David had yet to return.
So I strode out into the wake,
Into the fierce and white storm.
Lantern held high,
I trudged on through the snow.
Forcing my weary eye,
To search the horizon ever so slow.
I could not spot a thing,
From where I stood firm.
I decided I must bring,
Myself through the ice storm.
I fought my way high up the North Hill,
My lantern glowing dimly in the swirling flakes.
Not a thing around me was still,
Causing my eyes to waver in my traipse.
It was a long slow journey,
But I finally made it to the top.
Everything had begun to get real blurry,
And I had the feeling that I would soon drop.
The pain in my limbs faded,

To nothing more than a dull ache.
Before it disappeared and was traded,
To a numbness that I could not shake.
But never once did I fall,
To the cold, hard ground below.
I did not curl into a ball,
Though my heartbeat did slow.
It slowed until it finally,
Gave its final soft beat.
Leaving me frozen quietly,
And no longer able to greet.
I floated up,
Out of my body and into the gloomy sky.
Looking close-up,
I realized that this was how I would die.
My heart no longer beat,
My lungs no longer drew air.
There was not a bit of heat,
Left in this body to spare.
My limbs no longer moved,
I was at the end.
My muscles had all fused,
It was time for me to ascend.

The Bridge

Chapter Five

'There are very few monsters who warrant the fear we have of them.' -Andre Gide

Unlike you might think,
I did not know nothingness.
I did not disappear in a wink,
But instead become one with the darkness.
I did not ascend up high,
For I could not leave my baby behind.
I was not ready to say goodbye,
This I had to decline.
I floated above,
As nothing but the mist.
Wishing I could have gave my beloved,
One last kiss.
But the light did come,
Showing me the way I should go.
That was not the fate of a mum,
Who was needed back home through the snow.
So I did not follow the light,

Into the glory of the otherworld.
But stayed in the darkness of night,
Where the snow continued to swirl.
My journey was not yet finished,
I still had another path to walk.
A love that would never diminish,
For a child that could not yet talk.
Memories filled my spirit,
Pain filled my ghostly heart.
All because of a stupid visit,
To the North hill in the dark.
My lantern still flickered on,
A tiny beacon in the dark.
As the hours passed it shown,
Looking like a tiny spark.
I watched from up high,
As the doctor finally came.
He did not let my baby die,
But did not see my flickering flame.
I watched them as they treated my boy,
And saw that my husband was in good health.
But what diminished my joy,
Was that I had to do this all in stealth.
My baby could not feel as I kissed his head,
My David could not feel my hand.
My existence was now filled with dread,
The door to my life had been slammed.

But I could watch my little boy grow,
Even if it was from afar.
Even though,
I will be nothing but a misty star.
Tears slid slowly down my face,
As my new life sunk in.
I would forever be stuck in this place,
Where I could only watch my kin.
I made my choice,
And now I must exist.
There is nothing to rejoice,
Because I am not but mist.

I made my decision,
Now in this world I must stay.
Only being able to listen,
And be known as the lady in grey.
My husband grew worried,
And wondered why I was not there.
He ran out in a hurry,
Without a single care.
I floated above,
As he searched through the snow.
Wishing he could forgive,
Me for my thoughtless woe.
Then he saw the flicker,
So faint but there.

Up high on the hill that was bigger,
Than any climber would dare.
But I did,
And so did he.
Following the flicker that bid,
To the top like a silent plea.
He reached the top,
And dropped to his knees.
Cursing fate for the rob,
It had decided to seize.
He wept for my lost life,
And for the life we had yet to live.
Feeling as though someone had carved his heart out
with a knife,
Wishing I was still alive.

Resting my misty hand,
Upon his shoulder gently.
I would be damned,
If I could not tell him goodbye.
"You were the love of my life,
And Even into the next.
Release your internal strife,
For I am not vexed.
"I came out in the cold,
To find help for my son.
My body just could not hold,

On to the heat given to me by the sun.
"I love you and our boy,
And I will watch over you forever.
You were both my greatest joy,
And we have a bond that will never sever.
"I know you weep for me,
But you need not.
For I do not plead,
For the life that I have lost.
"I prayed for this,
And will never take it back.
I asked for the abyss
To lead me into the black.
"For my life in exchange for another,
Our son is here.
He may be without a mother,
But he has a life that did not disappear.
"I will miss you and love you,
And watch over you both forever.
I am gone that is true,
But this is something that you can weather.
"I give up my afterlife,
To watch over you both.
Within your life you will find laughter,
That will lead you through this growth.
"So do not cry for me,
My precious one.

You must agree,
That your life is nowhere near done."

The Church

Chapter Six

'Even death is not to be feared by one who has lived
wisely.'
-Buddha

That is not the end of my story,
While I am dead I am not gone.
It is not very cheery,
But it is something to which people are drawn.
I do not tell you this for pity,
Nor do I tell you this for fear.
I tell you this to acknowledge this tricky,
Little sphere.
Many years have passed,
Since the night I died.
Time has passed in a mass,
Of people, of roads, of life stretching wide.
But as the years pass,
One thing remains the same.
I stand atop of the hilltop grass,
With my tiny, flickering flame.

You see my figure,
Or my light.
As you gasp and whisper,
Wondering if you truly caught sight.
I don't do this to taunt,
But to show you that I am here.
I am one who haunts,
Dunvegan Park as it appears.
Struck down by a simple storm,
Twisting and blowing its chill.
Taking care of one I bore,
So that he would have a happy life to fill.
The Alberta storms are beautiful,
But deadly, it's true.
I have proved this irrefutable,
In all I have gone through.
The howling winds, and twirling snow,
Was no match for me.
So now I stand here in my glow,
Blinking in and out for you to see.
I am the North Hill ghost,
Now you know of me.
I do not say this to boast,
I just exist in these hills and trees.
But I am not the only one,
Who haunts these very grounds.
There is a story of a nun,

Who walks these hills up and down.
The second to tell her tale,
Will tell you of her life.
How she had taken the veil,
But had her life ended in strife.

The Cup Of Death

The Nun In The Hills

Chapter Seven

'We consume our tomorrows fretting about our
yesterdays.'
-Persius

I am not a wife or mother,
Nor am I a fancy Lady that is true.
But I am sort of a wife to another,
To the one I pray to at this pew.
A ghostly figure of white,
Still garbed in my habit.
Murdered for doing what was right,
It was as though I was wiped from the planet.
My name is Sister Mary,
And I am a nun of the church.
But my tale is far more scary,
One that was hidden from research.
I am the hidden secret,
Of one at Saint Charles Roman Catholic Mission.
One who discovered the treatment,
Of one with such evil ambition.

There is the evil of my murderer,
But also of the ones that hid his crimes.
A religion hid a murderer,
Wiping away all of the signs.
But I must start at the beginning,
At the place where it all started.
Even now my head is still spinning,
Over something not for the faint hearted.
I am the second ghost of Dunvegan Park,
Known by many around.
My story is quite dark,
For my death was a secret buried in the ground.
For you to understand my meaning,
You need to know the rest.
How a nun could have been brought such a demeaning,
Disgusting death.
The story will begin,
When I still lived and breathed.
When I lived within my own skin,
Before my life was regretfully seized.

The Ghost

Chapter Eight

'To pity distress is but human; to relieve it is Godlike.'
-Horace Mann

At a very young age,
I knew I was meant for God.
It never felt to me like a cage,
But a part of life that should be awed.
For a woman to give herself to the Lord,
Was a gracious and beautiful gift.
A life of being a nun who is adored,
Giving away nothing that I would have missed.
I had never craved a family of my own,
Or a house to cook and clean.
My calling was to the Lord upon the highest thrown,
Being a Catholic figurine.
Helping those poor and sick,
And those just needing the Lord.
Being the one that they would pick,
That they would come to and not be ignored.
I was an orphan child,

Who never really had a home.
I was unruly and wild,
Forever destined to roam.
Until I found the church,
And the beautiful sisters who raised me.
Ending my eternal search,
And helping me to finally be able to truly see.
See what I was meant for,
In this life to help other's needs.
To help others in the name of the Lord I swore,
Doing only good with my deeds.
As I grew I became a nun,
And took the habit in his name.
Feeling as though I had finally done,
That was my aim.
I was transferred and moved,
To the church in Dunvegan Park.
I wholeheartedly approved,
And felt like this is where I would finally spark.
I loved it all from the rolling hills and tall trees,
To the river below and surrounding plants.
I loved to walk along the hills and pick the many berries,
Or even the rosehips when I had the chance.
Father Marcus was our priest,
Who led us and showed us our way.
I had a feeling about him that never ceased,

That I could never truly slay.
"Young Sister Mary,
I greet you on this fine day."
Father Marcus's greeting was merry,
but my ill feeling would not be shoved away.
"Greeting Father,
I enjoy the beauty of this fine morn.
Before I find the doctor,
For some help about a baby about to be born.
"Mistress Janet has been laboring hard,
And I worry for her safety.
The Doctor may know a shard,
Of information that might help the baby."
"You should not wonder so far alone,
You should worry for yourself.
We would not wish for some unknown,
To harm you and cause an upset.
"I only tell you because I worry,
For the safety of all the sisters here.
Please do not be in such a hurry,
That you do not use a keen ear."
His hand resting upon my shoulder,
Made me cringe and flinch.
Wishing to just get away from the holder,
Where I would no longer feel the evil, creepy twinge.
"I will be careful,
But I really must go.

I am the Lord's vessel,
And I must get the doctor in tow."
I took a hasty step back,
And held up my hands toward him off.
"I really must get back on track,
This is nothing at which to scoff.
"The baby will soon be born,
The mother needs a helping hand.
I will not be the reason she must mourn,
Her baby if it must be buried in the sand.
"I must fetch the doctor quick,
So this must be farewell."
I said as I turned with a flick,
And ran before I gave into my need to yell.
It is true that I was a young woman,
And the terror might just be in my head.
But to me he seemed so inhuman,
With his interest in the dying and dead.
Maybe I overreacted,
He was a man of God.
But every time they interacted,
I could not help but believe him to be a fraud.

The Lady Of The Lake

Chapter Nine

'Were I called on to define, very briefly, the term Art, I should call it 'the reproduction of what the Senses perceive in Nature through the veil of the soul.' The mere imitation, however accurate, of what is in Nature, entitles no man to the sacred name of 'Artist."
-Edgar Allan Poe

My feeling about Father Marcus never changed,
This was not something that time could cure.
I just tried to make sure that we exchanged,
Not many words so that I felt secure.
But the uneasy feeling stayed,
And not because of the priest.
Women around the area had began to fade,
With no one knowing if they were alive or deceased.
Everyone felt on edge,
No one knew what to do.
We did not know how we had got to the ledge,
Where women were disappearing out of the blue.
"Oh, Sister Kate,

What shall we do?

Do we just wait,

Or do we wait until another is taken anew?

"I worry so for the ones who are lost,

Or are they even alive?

It started with the disappearance of the frost,

How are we to survive?

"Poor Mistress Janet and her baby,

They both disappeared last week.

I pray but maybe,

Fate is just very bleak."

"You should not speak that way."

Said Sister Kate with a scowl.

"The Lord is there, you just need to pray

And do not speak so fowl."

Sister Kate was the eldest sister there,

With wrinkles and a crooked back.

She had a nasty scowl and fierce glare,

That were like a silent attack.

And yet she did not make me cower,

Or shudder with confused fear.

Not like the power,

That the Father held oh so near.

I still had not figured out,

What repelled me from him so.

All I knew was that I had no doubt,

That he had some foe.

I knew not who it was,
Or even if there was more than one.
But the Father seemed to always give pause,
And his temper would go off like a gun.
"Have you noticed how Father Marcus does act,
Lately anytime someone questions him.
I don't want you to believe that I have snapped,
But he seems to be acting very grim.
"I do not mean to start a rumor,
I just try to be cautious.
He seems to be in such an ill humor,
I just don't want to be one of the losses."
"Father Marcus is so good to us,
He is the nicest priest we have had.
Why are you making such a fuss,
We you should be nothing but glad.
"We have had many priests before,
And none as kind as him.
He does not act as if we are some chore,
To be done with on a whim.
"I do not call him a Saint,
Nor do I call him our Savior.
But he utters almost no complaint,
And does not act as though he does us some great
favor.
"You should repent for your harsh thoughts,
And beg for his forgiveness.

You should be tied up in knots,
For thinking that he is sinless.
"He is not but a man,
Just the same as you and me.
He prays for his sin just as we can,
Hoping that with God's help it will flee.
"Pray for your soul young one,
For you are not sinless either.
You think the world should be all sun,
You are just a dreamer."
Sister Kate walked away,
Without another word.
Seeming to sway,
Under a secret that was stirred.
Now my curiosity was peeked,
But I didn't know what to do.
This secret seemed to have been leaked,
It seemed to involve more than a few.
Why did Sister Kate need to defend the Father,
When something felt so wrong.
I just felt so bothered,
At these feelings they were fighting so strong.
"I will find what they are hiding,
I do not care if that is a sin.
I will take all of their chiding,
I will find whatever they are engaged in.
"I will find their secret,

No matter how deep I have to dig.
I will not be impressed,
By the shields they shove up to trick.
"I will find what has happened to the women,
Where ever they might be.
I will find this dreadful villain,
And stop this crime spree.
"I refuse to be deterred,
From this path I choose.
I will make the lines of sin unblurred,
And make the culprit pay their dues."
Turning to walk the hills and think,
I picked berries as I went.
Thinking what would link,
These crimes to the Father's discontent.

The Lake

Chapter Ten

'While I thought that I was learning how to live, I have been learning how to die.' -Leonardo da Vinci

I followed the Father in secret,
Making not a single sound.
Hoping he would show the demon,
When no one else was around.
I followed him for weeks,
Hoping to catch a glimpse.
I didn't find what I seek,
For he was usually gone in a blink.
Try as I might to follow him again,
He lost me every time.
Making me scour the land in vane,
Hoping to catch some glimpse of the slime.
But I lost him time and time again,
And even more women disappeared.
Making me feel as if I was in part to blame,
For not catching the villain who was so feared.
But I refused to give up yet,

I needed to find these girls.
I would find this threat,
Before my life ended in a swirl.
What I never expected to find,
At Saint Charles Roman Catholic Mission.
I do not know how I could have been so blind,
What I found was as good as an admission.
One dark night I had an idea,
To retrace the steps of the Father that day.
I never expected there to be a,
A clue that could betray.
I did not dare to take a lantern,
Nor any light at all.
I was afraid the flickering pattern,
Would not look so very small.
I could not risk being caught,
Just to have a little light.
So I would have to find what I sought,
Using the moon on this dark night.
I followed the trail I had by day,
Through the winding weaving paths.
Searching the ground and trees along the way,
Past the creepy shadows of the night that were cast.
Then I heard a very faint sound,
A bare whisper through the hills.
I knew that I had somehow found,
The villain who gave me such chills.

I crept closer until I could finally see,
The villain as clear as day.
He stood by the river up to his knee,
With the dirt he dug and flung away.
As the dirt showered through the sky,
My eyes locked on the hole.
I gave a silent cry,
It was his horrible goal.
A hole dug six feet deep,
And large enough for a body.
That was when I caught a peep,
I saw it so lifeless and bloody.
I watched as the villain walked away,
And I made a sound of grief.
There left on display,
Were bodies by the reef.
Poor Mistress Janet,
And her tiny baby girl.
Were all bloody and damaged,
Their lives shattered like a priceless pearl.
The water that ran around their bodies,
Looked to be bleeding in sympathy.
But water could not copy,
It was their lives turning the water red visibly.
Tears ran silently down my cheeks,
As I crept to the bodies and started to weep.
Those poor girls had been missing for weeks.

And now they were gone and pilled in a heap.
They looked as though they had been tortured,
Slashes and cuts gracing their pale skin.
Janet's arm looked to be fractured,
And the poor baby's life had just started to begin.
The person who did this was sick,
And loved to see others in pain.
Who liked to take life so quick,
And torture a person until they were no longer sane.
That was when I heard the noise,
The hushed whisper of voices.
It must have been the villain who enjoys,
Making others voiceless.
I crept back up to my hiding place,
And watched from where I was hidden.
That was when I saw the faces,
Of the ones who did something so forbidden.
Father Marcus and Sister Kate's faces were so clear,
In the moonlight shining down.
Upon their faces they both held a sneer,
Not shocked at all to see dead bodies around.
Then I heard their voices with a clarity,
As they discussed what they had done.
Talking as though this was not some rarity,
And as if there was a battle that they had just won.
"You must pray over they bodies now,
And wash away the sin.

So that the Lord will allow,
Their afterlife to begin.
"Do not give me that look,
You know as well as I.
We have not mistook,
The signs we have seen from our ally.
"They had to die,
Just like the others.
All they did was defy,
And so they were forced to suffer.
"We do this for the one true God,
And the sinners as is his will.
If all knew of our actions they would applaud,
That we do so much good still.
"Now grab the shovel,
And bury them deep.
Then we must grovel,
For their souls that will reap."
They each grabbed a shovel,
And buried the two.
Hurrying as though the devil,
Was coming for what he was due.
They prayed over the grave,
Of the people they had killed.
As though that would save,
Their lives which evil had filled.
I watched them leave,

And I ran to the grave to weep.
Feeling that they deserved someone to grieve,
Their lives which the loss seemed steep.
I did not hear a sound,
But suddenly everything was black.
The two had come back around,
And given me a solid whack.
They drug my body high on the hill,
Where I walked to pick my berries.
They then threw my body downhill,
Hoping in the river I would be buried.
While the toss down the hillside killed me,
In the waters I was not concealed for long.
Washed up on the shore for all to see,
But they found nothing wrong.
'A simple stumble',
'She was dumb to walk in the dark'.
'I must have been troubled',
'Or possibly off to do Gods work'.
What they did not know,
Was that I still saw them all.
Walking my hills in woe,
And hate for the ones that caused my fall.

The Liar

Chapter Eleven

'If you don't have any fight in you, you might as well be dead.'
-Scott Caan

He should have suffered for what he had done,
But that was not meant to be.
They called it the mysterious circumstances of the nun,
They did not link me to the killing spree.
I rose from my body,
As a dark grey mass.
Wishing that somebody,
Would find what I had seen at last.
The light shone bright,
And the heavens beckoned me.
But I had to stay and fight,
Because I was not free.
I was one of the lost souls,
That were killed by the monster.
Buried in deep holes,

Or given to the water.
My work in this world was not done yet,
I needed to stop the pair.
I needed to make sure there was no longer a threat,
From people that most were not aware.
So I stayed in this world,
And learned to be a ghost.
Making sure that my image flickered and swirled,
So that my death was not one that they could boast.
I stayed in this world by choice,
While the others were trapped.
Wanting to give all the victims a voice,
Until they could find a way to attack back.
Some of the others were scared,
While most just felt anger.
Hating the ones that smeared,
Their names and weighed their bodies down like
anchors.
I walked the hills along my trails,
Picking berries and rosehips as I went.
Wavering my image so that there would be tales,
Of the ghost nun who needed to vent.
I made sure Father Marcus saw me,
And Sister Kate too.
All they wanted to do was flee,
To run from what they were due.
But they could leave,

Without saying why.
So on every eve,
They were forced to see their lie.
It drove them mad,
One after the other.
So they did what they thought they had,
And killed one another.
Father Marcus killed the sister,
Ended her life real quick.
He gave her a draft that was bitter,
Then blew out her life like a candles burning wick.
Then to end his own,
He found a brew to smother.
That would make him cough and groan,
Until he fell asleep with a shudder.
I found it very cruel,
That their crimes were never learned.
That souls were forever ruined,
And lives were left to burn.
I may not be an angered spirit,
But many of the others are.
With that anger comes the appearance,
Comes a more hateful being from hell's fiery char.
So while you have nothing to fear from me,
You do from the others.
Leave them to fume in peace or we,
Become the nightmares from which you hide under

the covers.

The Map

Chapter Twelve

'Of all the gods only death does not desire gifts.' -
Aeschylus

There deaths were seen as sickness,
Their lives all but adored.
No one saw the mental illness,
Their vows they seemed to ignore.
The souls of the lost are not all lying here,
Where I now make my home.
Some decided to disappear,
Because they felt no need to roam.
They went into the light,
Releasing all of their loathing and hate.
Not wanting to be figures that fright,
Deciding to cross over the gate.
While my killers are dead,
I am still here.
Through my trails I tread,
Picking berries and rosehips that are near.
Many have watched as I walk my paths,

Wishing to know my story.
Seeing my ghostly figure as it casts,
No shadow in its horror.
I do not tell my story to cast,
Fear into your heart.
I just wish you to know how my life was smashed,
And why I walk this part.
I am the nun on the hill,
Now you finally know.
How the monsters did kill,
Me and created this woe.
My murderers do not walk here,
At least they have not been seen,
But we are ghosts that disappear,
So they could easily be somewhere in the green.
I pray that they were drug to hell,
Where they could suffer for all time.
But I know that they could be that frightening yell,
That hides in the dark waiting to commit another
crime.
So tread carefully in this land,
Because not all spirits are good.
You might anger a dead hand,
That would kill you if it could.
But I am only the second,
There are still others to tell.
Of other essences that beckon,

Who live here as well.
The next story of Dunvegan Park,
Is of another priest.
His story will lead you to embark,
On a journey that never ceased.

The Mask Of Good

The Priest In The Rectory

Chapter Thirteen

'Death most resembles a prophet who is without
honor in his own land or a poet who is a stranger
among his people.'
-Khalil Gibran

I am another ghost of Dunvegan Park,
Whom haunts these hallowed grounds
I am the ones whose vision will spark,
As I make my rounds.
I was not a father or a husband,
But one of the leaders of this mission.
One who did as he was summoned,
Without any suspicion.
My name is Father Paul,
I was a priest in Dunvegan Park.
My story is in these hallowed halls,
That hold some secrets that are dark.
I saw something that was never meant to be,
For that my life was ended.
After seeing that I could not pretend to not see,

Or take the offer that was extended.
But as one of the Lord's loyal servants,
I was give some power.
To show others of my purpose,
After my deathly hour.
But for you to learn my meaning,
We must first begin with life.
And how my intervening,
Caused a terrible strife.
The story will begin,
When I still lived and breathed.
When I lived within my own skin,
Before my life was regretfully seized.

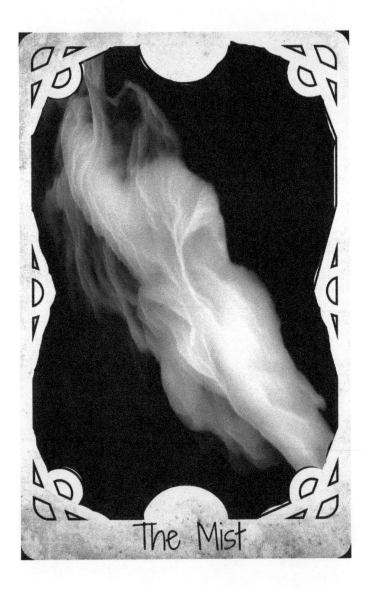

The Mist

Chapter Fourteen

'Death is the cure for all diseases.' -Thomas Browne

I was a younger son,
Whom was destined for the church.
This destiny was my one,
And I found that I loved the research.
I became an illuminator,
One who researched and read.
I was the new communicator,
Between the church and the people we led.
I love books,
English and Latin alike.
I read them over with many looks,
There was nothing that I ever disliked.
I was happy will my pages and words,
That filled my life so full.
I was working my way towards,
Learning everything that I could pull.
It was a good life,
And I enjoyed my post at Dunvegan Park.

But there was no way I saw the strife,
That I was about to find in the dark.
I looked up from my desk in shock,
When Brother Mario stepped into my room.
He did not usually come to talk,
When I was with my books consumed.
"I need you to look some things over,
Before you turn in for the night.
I need you to read these letters,
And tell me what they did write."
I took the papers from him,
And looked them over with care.
The ink was very dim,
But you could tell that an old language was written there.
"Why do you have these letters,
Filled with a language unused.
You are supposed to deal with the beggars,
Not read letters whose truth is unproved."
"Your job is not to question,
But to illuminate what you are brought.
This is your profession,
So do as you were taught."
Brother Mario snapped,
Throwing the letters onto the desk.
I felt as though my knuckles had been rapped,
Then he backed away as though I was something

grotesque.
With a huff of impatience,
I looked at the letters he threw.
I could not help the anticipation,
Within me that grew.
It was like this anytime I found a new challenge,
I was giddy and impatient.
I loved the look of knew knowledge,
Especially one so ancient.
I ran my finger over the pages,
So tattered and aged.
Feeling a little gracious,
For having these letters to engage.
It was like looking in to another time,
Before I was even born.
Being able to read through this grime,
To read the pages that were so worn.
So I set to work,
And deciphered the letters.
My eyes widened at what they did mark,
That they were written by my betters.
What was Brother Mario into,
That he needed to know these words.
He dealt with the beggars so why would he intrude,
And how would he come to have a letter from the
lords.
As I read deeper into the letters,

I found that they were not so old.
They used this ancient language going to great
measures,
To hide something as precious as gold.
Secrets that they wished to remain hidden,
And thought to be ancient and lost.
Of things that are forbidden,
And the lives that it could cost.
As I read deeper into the stories,
I began to tremble in fear.
At first they seemed like entries in diaries,
But now it was becoming quite clear.
While they were written like it only had one author,
Looking closely at the words I could see that there
was another.
They wrote of their joyous prosper,
And of how the smell of blood grows stronger.
I wondered why they spoke of blood,
But I saw it again and again in the writing.
They spoke of something called the 'flood',
And how the sight of it was so exciting.
I soon realized that the authors were women,
Who drained others of their life's fluid.
Who enjoyed the look and smell of the crimson,
And yet did not see their actions as cruel.
They were sick and twisted beings,
Who needed to be stopped.

I did not know why Brother Mario was in such dealings,
Whose actions completely shocked.
I pushed the pages away in disgust,
Wishing that I could throw them in the fire to burn.
This was something that I had never wished to discuss,
And I never would as far as this was concerned.

The North Hill

Chapter Fifteen

'Someone has to die in order that the rest of us should value life more.' -Virginia Woolf

"What have you learned from my papers,
What have you read in them?
I have called up many favors,
To get possession of these beautiful gems."
Brother Mario startled me,
As he came slamming into my room.
It was not worded as a question or plea,
But more as a demand filled with gloom.
"I cannot help you I am sorry,
But this is a language that is dead from no use.
This is something even I cannot unbury,
It is too old to deduce."
A part of me felt bad for the lie,
But it had to be told.
I could not let him know why,
I could not tell him the words that were so cold.
I did not know why I had this distrust,

But I did and I knew I could not trust him.
This was something that could not be discussed,
It was just something too horrible and grim.
"You lie,
I know you do!
I just do not know why,
But I will promise you,
"That I will find what is written in those,
No matter what your wishes.
I will know all that those letters disclose,
This will be my mission."
"You will have to do that with some other letters,
I seemed to have misplaced the ones you gave.
But I tell you that you will never,
Understand the language that those letters gave."
Brother Mario left the room in a huff,
And I knew that at least for now I had won.
I gave a sigh of relief at my working bluff,
But I knew that this was far from done.
I did not know why,
I felt I needed to hide this from him.
There were just things that did not comply,
So it was safest to keep him dim.
Checking to make sure that the coast was clear,
I took out the letters once more.
I needed to know what was feared,
What they did that was so deplored.

So I started to read the words spelled clear,
And found things that made me gasp in horror.
These disgusting witch's thought that is was dear,
To drain blood from another with a borer.
They spoke of draining virgins,
Who were beautiful and sweet.
Acting like home surgeons,
The sight of blood making their hearts beat.
They drained the blood into a large tub,
And filled it to the rim.
Then they would get in and scrub,
It would make their skin glisten instead of dim.
"They bored holes in these innocent women,
Just to bath in their blood.
That is completely insane,
Do they not see that as a dud?
"How can the blood of another make you younger,
Or give you eternal life?
They seem to have this evil hunger,
This need to slice with a knife.
"But where does Brother Mario fit into this,
Why does he wish to know?
Is he perhaps an accomplice,
Or does he too wish for this glow?"
I pondered this all,
But I knew I must find.
The names by which these women were called,

And do something to get them confined.
I read through the pages,
Searching word by word.
Reading through the exchanges,
Until coming across something I had earlier ignored.
My dearest, sweet Lizzie
I long for the blood once more.
The wrinkles and pale skin have come easy,
My good looks I do mourn.
My Lady Seewald,
I found ones who are perfect.
Our beauty will no longer be stalled,
The Brother brings them for us to collect.
The 'Brother',
She capitalizes the word as though it is not a sibling.
It could have been another,
But I have this feeling that is niggling.
Why else would he be so angry and anxious,
To find what was written.
He should not have been conscious,
Of the script that was hidden.
Then there were the two names that slipped,
Lady Seewald and Lizzie too.
That was when I knew that they had tripped,
And found what would bring them into view.
There was only Lady Isabelle Seewald around these
parts,

And she had a cousin Elizabeth Smith.
These had to be the Queens of corpses,
The ones who should only be a myth.
But I could not prove that as a fact,
Until I had cold hard proof.
I was going to have to track,
The two who were so aloof.
I will find them to condemn,
And in the process I will watch Brother Mario with great care.
If he is in league with them,
He will not be spared.
I may be a man of God,
But I will not tolerate evil.
Our system may be a little flawed,
But we are not medieval.
We do not harm others,
And we certainly do not kill.
We do not take pleasure while others suffer,
We do only good with our skill.
At least that is what we are taught to do,
While others lose their way.
But I will make sure they get what they are due,
They will be punished for those that they slay.

The Note

Chapter Sixteen

'Because I could not stop for death, He kindly stopped for me; The carriage held but just ourselves and immortality.'
-Emily Dickinson

I searched the pages,
And followed the women in secret.
But I found no basis,
And no hint of an inner demon.
But it had to be there,
So I continued to look.
When I saw something rare,
And that I almost mistook.
It was just a single glance between the two,
After the morning mass.
A look that gave me a clue,
On what was about to pass.
It was not a look between the cousins,
But between Brother Mario and the Lady.
A look that was very sudden,

But was terribly shady.
I did not know what it meant,
But I was going to find out.
I would find where they did this evil descent,
And how it all had come about.
I watched Brother Mario closely,
Well into the night.
When suddenly he began to act boldly,
And tried to scurry away from sight.
I followed silently in the darkness,
Not making a single sound.
It was easy on this night that was starless,
To follow him up to the compound.
I watched him walk through the night,
And enter the house of screams.
The house that made them all feel fright,
A place no one had lived in for years it seems.
He entered through the door,
While I stayed behind,
It was not long before,
The screams and the wind entwined.
Blood curdling screams,
That sent a shiver down my spine.
Not even in my most horrible dreams,
Had I ever crossed that bloody line.
The line between man and beast,
That every being seemed to fight.

For the beast would bring you to a bloody feast,
While the man would always see the light.
This was the line that had been crossed,
By others but not I.
They delivered souls that were lost,
Into a gruesome demise.
I did not have to see,
To know the torture that went on behind closed doors.
Now I had my proof on the three,
To bring justice to what was ignored.
I made my way back to my room,
And began to write.
A letter that would bring about their doom,
As soon as it was light.
A hand suddenly grabbed my shoulder,
And swung me around.
Forcing me to face the holder,
It would seem that I had been found.
I was now forced to face,
The three I tried to convict.
They must have gave chase,
and they seem to have come well equipped.
A rope dangled from Lizzie's arm,
A letter and flowers were grasped in Isabelle's hand.
But it was Brother Mario who did alarm,
For he held a gag as though this was all planned.
He shoved it in my mouth,

Before I had a chance to scream.
Isabelle laid the flowers north to south,
While Lizzie tied a noose and hung it to the beam.
"You were dumb to follow me tonight,
And even dumber for keeping our letters.
Now you have forced our might,
Because you thought you were so clever.
"I thought you were like me,
That you wished for eternal life.
I had thought that you would agree,
And help us keep our lives by taking others with a knife.
"But I was wrong,
And now you sit here to convict.
Us for what we have done all along,
And take away the beauty that we can inflict.
"But the others too are getting suspicious,
So I decided to kill two birds with one stone.
We wrote a letter of you confessing your sickness,
And of how you have felt so alone.
"Then in your fear and sadness,
You take your worthless life from this reality.
They will all finally see your madness,
And how it was a good thing that you took your mortality.
"It will explain the many that have disappeared,
So we will no longer have to worry.

We will be all but cleared,
And carry on in our flurry.
"But to do this I am sorry but you must die,
You will hang in this very room.
Oh and you won't move because I was quite sly,
I placed a paralysis poison on your gag that you have
now consumed."
That was when I noticed,
That I could not fight back.
I could not even protest,
Or do any harm to this pack.
I knew them that I would truly die,
There was nothing I could do.
So I braced myself and gave a silent goodbye,
I just wished I could have stopped them before this
was what it came to.
I kept my eyes wide open,
Wanting them to watch what they were doing.
That was when my life was stolen,
My neck broken and my lips already bluing.
I rose from my body,
And saw they were as happy as can be.
I had hoped that they would at least be sorry,
And feel some guilt over their killing spree.
But that was not to happen,
So I sat at my desk.
Hoping that my talent,

Would come out as something helpful and good
instead of grotesque.
Somehow it did,
And my quill picked up in my hand.
So I wrote on my parchment to help this world get
rid,
Of the three who tormented this land.
I felt the pull of the otherworld,
But my mission was not yet done.
I could not go to the underworld,
Until this game was won.
My body was found the very next day,
But so too was my note.
The constable went to the manor to make them pay,
But the mob had already taken a vote.
They locked the three,
Within the house of screams.
And set it ablaze for all to see,
To take the nightmares away from the dreams.

The Nun

Chapter Seventeen

'I had seen birth and death but had thought they were different.' -T. S. Eliot

This story was not written in the history books,
But hidden as a shame.
Taking away the existence of the virgins with looks,
Who were killed because of a sick game.
The three killers,
Were also struck from the records.
Erasing the sinners,
From every single report.
Then there was me,
Who too was erased.
Taking away the good I had done with glee,
All because my death was debased.
That is why I haunt here still,
Never leaving the rectory.
I sit here with my parchment and quill,
Because I was left as no more than a memory.
It was wrong for them to destroy,

Our lives as though we were naught.
Robbing us of the joy,
Of generation knowing of how we fought.
But the history of our lives died with us,
Because of the sins of three.
Our lives they will never discuss,
All because of a killing spree.
So now I am seen as a ghost,
Who haunts the old Dunvegan rectory.
Seen at the window by most,
But also seen at my desk in my memory.
For I am a powerful being,
Who can project the room as it was?
And have the living seeing,
Me in this pause.
So now you know my tale,
And why it is not widely known.
How I was able to avail,
Even in the death in to which I was thrown.
I do not tell this for sympathy,
Or for hatred of the ones whom erased us.
I tell this to simply,
To keep our memory discussed.
 I am the priest in the rectory,
Who was erased from the past.
Who is naught but a faded memory,
Because of killers who harassed.

But there is one more,
Whose story must be heard.
She is the Lady we adore,
Whose history is often blurred.
She is the Lady On The River,
And her tale is as old as time.
It is one she will deliver,
And is so sublime.
She is the guardian of us all,
Who keeps us good and pure.
Because we did not heed the light's call,
She makes sure that we do not cave to evil's allure.

The Pict

The Lady Of The Lake

Or

The Lady Of The River

Or

The Woman On The Bridge

Chapter Eighteen

'Death is a fearful thing.' -William Shakespeare

They call me the Lady of the River,
But also the Lady on the Bridge.
But what I am is much bigger,
When the waters completely filled this ditch.
Crystal clear blue,
As far as the eye could see.
The Lady of the Lake is how I was viewed,
Protecting all those who needed me.
I am the figure of mist,
Dressed in a hooded cloak and bare feet.
I am seen and then dismissed,
The one you are never sure if you actually meet.
I was first seem when the bridge was finished,
But that was not when I died.
My life was ended centuries before the water
diminished,
To nothing more than a hilly prairie with a river
beside.

But I was not always this hooded figure,
Who walks in the mist upon the water.
I am this because of a self-righteous killer,
Who led me to my slaughter.
This was many years ago,
Before Dunvegan Park was even here.
When this was naught but a blue lake with a beautiful
glow,
So deep that you could just disappear.
But to know me true,
You must learn of my past.
When I was regretfully slew,
By someone I would have thought of last.
My history is not written in any book that you will
find,
In part it has to do with the name this place has today.
It is the place the settle people of my kind,
And kept our enemies at bay.
Many have heard of the magic of Skye,
Well this was the Skye of this land.
And this was the magical lake where I died,
Before it drained because of a glacier that was
unplanned.
But to know my tale,
You must first learn of my lifetime.
How I did sail,
From daylight to nighttime.

The story will begin,
When I still lived and breathed.
When I lived within my own skin,
Before my life was regretfully seized.

The Priest

Chapter Nineteen

'To have died once is enough.' -Virgil

I was not a mother nor was I married,
And I never chose to be.
I was not a nun nor harried,
But a woman of the sea.
The water was always my calling,
Just as it is with many of my kind.
My lake was so calming,
And more beautiful than you would ever find.
My name is Viviane,
I am the lady of the lake.
I am one of the blessed women,
Is the guide of these waters that quake.
We were a family of Picts,
That came from across the great seas.
Our skin was marked with blue script,
And we possessed such gifts that made our souls fly
free.
I was the youngest of my family,

Seven daughters in total.
Our mother was so lucky,
For she was given the proposal.
All seven of us would take the test,
For one of us was the seer.
Who would be the guardian of those on a quest,
Would guide the boat here.
There was always one guardian,
To protect the others of our kind.
My grand-mama was the last who guarded,
But the mists would no longer bind.
To explain what my kind are,
And what we are taught to do.
I must tell you that we came from far,
Across the seas we blew.
We were a part of the true hidden Skye,
But we were sailors true.
So we sailed so far to try,
A new home too.
We landed but it was not enough,
So we traveled farther land.
Then we came upon a bluff,
And found a lake so grand.
We paddled across the crystal blue,
And found a home on the other side.
A place that nobody knew,
And was safe for us to hide.

For each one of us possess a skill,
That most people do fear.
Some controlled the heat or chill,
While others could sense emotions so mere.
But the most sacred of all of the gifts,
The control over the waters and mists.
So with each generation the power shifts,
To the new girls which has the powers that exist.
There must always be one,
In a generation.
Or our shield will be undone,
And we will be doomed to damnation.
For the ones without powers,
Think that we are evil because we are different.
They would kill us as we cowered,
All because they are ignorant.
My grand-mama was old and tired,
Crooked with age.
She was ready to retire,
And pass on to her life's next stage.
But first another must be found,
So my sisters and I were the first to be tried.
To sense our surrounds,
And attempt a shield to hide.
My sisters all went first,
Controlling air, fire, earth, sound, gravity, heat and
cold as they went.

But none of them were able to make the shield enforced,
But now it was my turn to show my powers to their extent.
I took a deep breath and held my hands before me,
Summoning up my powers to explode.
For the longest moment nothing happen that anyone could see,
And then it suddenly flowed.
I could hear the gasps around,
So opened my eyes to see.
The mists had grown so much that they began to surround,
The town and all the trees.
I glanced to my grand-mama,
And saw her smiling gleefully.
Everyone was happy that I fulfilled the promise,
And kept us in our secrecy.
"You are the one I waited for,
My little Viviane.
Now it is your turn to do this chore,
And keep us in oblivion.
"I will teach you all that you need to learn,
Before my time comes to an end.
But be warned my child even though you might yearn,
This side you must defend.

"The others would harm all that we are,
In our peaceful existence.
Remember we are children of a far,
And we live because of our persistence.
"You must never bring one of them to our side,
For it will surely end in gore.
This is where we must reside,
Or that is what you will answer for."
I was a mere age of seven,
When this chore passed down to me.
Causing me to question,
If we were actually free.

The River

Chapter Twenty

'Death is the last enemy: once we've got past that I think everything will be alright.' -Alice Thomas Ellis

I aged and learned all that I could,
And now I was a beautiful eighteen.
With hair the color of the richest wood,
And eyes a leafy green.
A long lean body and pump cherub cheeks,
With lips stained the brightest red.
I was a beauty that bespeaks,
Of something that is only read.
In my time as the seer,
I had earned my Pict marks too.
With each blue tattoo that appeared,
I felt as though I was being born anew.
For with greater wisdom,
My markings came.
Making me feel a sense of heroism,
For protecting those that I claimed.
But with age also came curiosity,

At what was on the other side.
Was it truly a monstrosity,
Or was that where my dreams hide.
So each day as the sunset turned the world to night,
I dawned my white cloak and set off in my boat.
Creating an opening in my curtain to paddle towards
a new sight,
And sit on that side of the shield afloat.
I never touched my bare feet to the grass,
Still worried about what my grand-mama warned.
But needing to see this land that I often pass,
But kept on the waters where I could not be harmed.
I did this every night for a fortnight,
Before I spotted the man.
I saw it as good fortune,
To see him across the span.
He sat upon the ground,
And stared straight at me.
I then knew that I was bound,
To set foot on the other side quickly.
He was so handsome,
All that was golden and bright.
Built like a cannon,
And he sat there looking like a white knight.
He waved me over,
And I found myself paddling close.
He sat serenely in a patch of clover,

And with a single look I chose.
"Why do you sit there,
Every single night?
Looking at the land and stare,
Until the beginning of first light."
His voice was a soft rumble,
That was pleasant to the ear.
I brought my chin up and in a voice with a hint of a
tremble,
I spoke loud and clear.
"What is your name?"
I asked across the waters.
"And why do you claim,
As though you have seen me here before?"
"I am called Arthur here,
And I have seen you come from the mist.
I have watched you for many nights just disappear,
As though for you the mists shift."
My heart pounded hard in my chest,
As I reached the shore and placed a single barefoot
upon the grassy incline.
She did not know what possessed,
Why she did something that could killed the ones she
left behind.
I drew my hood down,
And stared down at this intriguing man.
"Your hair is a beautiful crown,

Your skin sun kissed and tan.
"The marks upon your skin are precious,
As though there are rivers running beneath.
I have never seen anything so breathless,
Their beauty wrapping around you like a sheath.
"Your eyes shimmer like green gems,
Your lips are like a blooming rose.
Even with your air of mystery I cannot condemn,
Because I am one that knows.
"How hard it is to fit in,
With your family and friends.
I do not relate to my own kin,
But for you I would go to the world's ends.
"Yes you are beautiful,
But I also sense something more.
For you are a woman of fable,
One who I could live with and adore."
As he spoke,
He stepped closer still.
Releasing the tie on my white cloak,
As he brushed his fingers across my cheek with a
thrill.
We sat upon the grassy knoll,
And talked into the night.
To each other we bared our souls,
And felt our bond so tight.
But every good thing,

Must come to its end.
The rays of the day began to spring,
We had no more time to spend.
With a final goodbye kiss,
That was so soft and sweet.
I promised to return to this bliss,
Every night for us to meet.

The Truth

Chapter Twenty-One

'In the night of death, hope sees a star, and listening love can hear the rustle of a wing.' -Robert Green Ingersoll

I went back every night,
And we grew closer each time.
But I suffered from this internal fight,
For doing something that was seen as a crime.
I was risking my people,
Simply for a pretty face.
I began feeling evil,
For risking those I protected from chase.
I was given one rule,
And have broken it time and time again.
Was I just being a fool,
Would these feelings wane?
I felt so confused,
But I kept going back.
I gave myself excuses,
But I began to feel the lack.

Arthur always wished to talk of me,
And the powers that I possess.
But he was never free,
With himself when I would press.
I do not know what to trust,
My brain or my heart.
But I knew that we must,
From now on be apart.
"I have to call this to its end,
I am breaking our most sacred rule.
No longer can I bend,
To the will of my heart like a fool.
"I have loved our time together,
But we could never be.
To my world I am tethered,
I can no longer flee.
"You have no future to offer,
Nor have you spoken of such.
I cannot lead my people to slaughter,
Nor can I allow yours to be jury and judge.
"I hope that you can understand,
Why this must be our final goodbye.
This has not happened as I had planned,
I can no longer look my people in the eye and lie."
He trailed his fingers across my cheek,
And gave me a soft smile.
He was what she did seek,

With looks that did beguile.
"I care for you Viviane,
But I cannot promise you much.
Before you disappear into oblivion,
Meet me tomorrow for one last touch.
"I will wait for you here,
In our spot that is so special.
The place where no one can overhear,
Us if we are careful.
"I just need one more night,
Before we part ways.
We should do this right,
If it will be our last day.
"Please tell me yes,
That we shall meet.
Or I will obsess,
That this was our last time to talk and greet."
I thought over his suggestion,
And thought that it could do no harm.
It might help halt my questions,
On whether I was in love with him or his charm.
I nodded my head,
And gave him a little grin.
Hoping that it would not be misread,
Or cause him to feel chagrin.
"We will meet again on the morrow,
Beneath these stars once more.

And then we will part with sorrow,
For this is the end, I swore."
I got into my little boat,
And rowed home again.
Tomorrow would be the final note,
Of the relationship I must abstain.
I could no longer lie,
To the people who relied on me so.
I could no longer ally,
Myself with those on the other side of the shields
glow.
I would heed my grand-mama's words,
And protect the others of my kind.
I would do my job as the guard,
To these waters I would bind.

The River Of Red

Chapter Twenty-Two

'I think what weakens people most is fear of wasting their strength.' -Etty Hillesum

I brushed my hair until it shone,
And put on my finest silk gown.
This was the last time I would row out alone,
Before our relationship would be burned down.
If this was to be the last I see of my love,
I would look my very best.
I would for once look the part of the dove,
There would be nothing about me that he could attest.
"Where do you go young one,
On a storm so stormy with gloom?"
My Grand-mama asked as I spun,
To face her in the room.
"I cannot tell,
It is my business."
I forced out as I felt spelled,
To tell her the truth that very minute.
Her aged eyes held mine,

And I watched them glaze over with knowing.
On the lies that did twine,
About me so I now felt them choking.
"You have broken the rule,
And set foot on the other side."
She held up her hand, "Do you think me a fool?
That I cannot see clearly what you try to hide?"
"You do not understand, Grand-mama."
I pleaded my case.
"I do love him and I promise,
He would never harm any of us in this place.
"Arthur is sweet and loving,
But I have called it to an end.
For I cannot stand the guilt rubbing,
I can no longer pretend.
"I know that I place everyone at risk,
Because of my selfishness.
Our relationship was sweet but brisk,
For I will not sentence everyone here to
helplessness."
A grin touched Grandmama's lips,
As she stepped forwards to give me a fierce hug.
"I am glad you have come to grips,
On your own before I had time to judge.
"I know how hard it is to stay away from temptation,
After all my first child was born of an outsider.
But even one of them who is a relation,

Can turn on us with hatred in their every fiber.
"I know you go to meet you man tonight,
For the final time.
But do not be fooled into thinking that he is your knight,
Because he has the ability to commit a horrible crime.
"He would not hesitate to destroy us all,
Where would your love be then?
Your back would be up against a wall,
You would be forced to choose a side, them or the glen."
I knew all she said was true,
But my heart still broke to pieces.
I was being forced to change my life's view,
My love I was forced to release.
"I choose the glen,
Before I cause any pain.
I love our peaceful den,
And I refuse to watch the lives in it drain.
"I am the lady of the lake,
I am the guardian of this valley.
It is my destiny to create,
To keep us shielded gently.
"I know that I must listen to my brain,
That tells me that something is not quite right.
What I feel for him will most likely wane,
But I must give him one last night."

"I understand that my dear granddaughter,
I just ask that you be careful.
Use wisdom and the power of the water,
And always travel barefoot.
"Your power comes from the water,
And the beauty that is the mist.
With that you may destroy any fodder,
That would light and destroy us very swift.
"But remember that you are not just your powers,
But a person as well.
That would scale any tower,
To protect this place that we dwell.
"I know you will do the right thing,
Even though it is hard.
Beware not to bring,
The wrath of the others that can only be feared.
"But before you leave,
I have one more question to ask.
You fell in love but did you conceive,
For I understand how one and lead to the parenting
task."
I paused for a moment,
Knowing the truth but not wanting to say.
It was not enough that my love would be stolen,
But a child had begun to weigh.
How would I tell the man of my heart,
That I was with child but we could not be?

For its safety we would have to be apart,
His child he could never see.
The look in my Grand-mama's eyes,
Told me that she had guessed the truth.
That she had seen through guise,
And that no words were needed to soothe.
She saw me for what I was,
But was not disappointed or shamed.
There was an understanding that I had broken our laws,
But for that my child would not be blamed.
That was the end of our silent communication,
It was time for me to have my final meeting.
It was time to go to my haven,
And halt my hearts rapid beating.
My heart would be ripped to pieces,
Within a single night.
But I was doing what was needed,
To keep our people from an age old fight.

The Unmarked Grave

Chapter Twenty-Three

*'I am convinced that it is not the fear of death, of our
lives ending that haunts our sleep so much as the
fear... that as far as the world is concerned, we might
as well never have lived.' -Harold Kushner*

Just as I had done for many nights before,
I rowed out on the lake and past my glowing shield.
Then made my way to the shore,
Where my fate would be sealed.
As I set a barefoot upon the other side,
I noticed that Arthur was not waiting as usual.
Why would he not be seated by the low tide,
Where we could say goodbye to something beautiful?
So I sat upon his spot,
And waited for him to come.
Knowing that he would not have forgot,
About this like some.
I would wait the entire night,
If it meant I could see him just once.
He was my white knight,

It was not just a front.
Suddenly my world went dark,
As I was struck from behind.
But I came to with a spark,
And a gasp as I cleared my mind.
I was laying upon the ground,
Surrounded by a group of men.
I gazed all around,
And I saw him then.
Within the group stood my Arthur,
Looking so cruel and mean.
Dress all up in his armor,
It no longer held a white sheen.
No longer was he my knight in white,
But an evil being dressed in red.
This was the real him who he held away from the
light,
The man who was the reason that many were dead.
You could see it in the way he held himself,
And even the stain of his armor.
He did well with pretend,
I wished I had listened to the murmur.
The one that warned me deep inside,
Of the dangers I did court.
The one that told me what could hide,
Behind the face of my handsome consort.
"What do you here Arthur?

Why have you betrayed me like this?
And why do you harbor,
These killers from the abyss?"
I snapped at the leader,
As I recognized the other men.
They were the crew who were so eager,
For the blood of those who resided in the glen.
They were murderers and thieves,
Cutthroats and bandits.
Led by their beliefs,
Of returning the world to its balance.
A balance that didn't involve,
The existence of people with gifts.
They believed we could enthrall,
Others to jump off cliffs.
Every bad thing in the world,
They blamed on us.
Saying that the threads of the world unfurled,
That this was not just mistrust.
To them Picts were the devil,
Just waiting for their moment to strike.
To them we were a venom,
And our heads needed to be upon pikes.
But they were lies they told themselves,
To give an excuse for the lives they had taken.
Killing is how they excel,
Making sure my kind never again awakens.

"You were a fool to think I cared,
About you or any of your worthless kind.
You are nothing compared,
To the wife I have left behind."
Arthur sneered in glee,
As he gloated about my capture.
But I refused to cry and plea,
It didn't matter that he was my captor.
"You went to great lengths,
To destroy me and my kind.
But you could not see the strength,
That I had hidden and confined.
"I fought with myself,
Not knowing what to do.
But now I am happy I chose to protect,
My kind and my daughter from you."
There was a moment of shocked silence,
Before Arthur sneered.
"You may be some young siren,
But you do not have a daughter who is adored."
"I may not yet have her here,
But she grows every day.
She will be the good from my horrible year,
That came from being with someone so insane."
There was once more silence,
As he took this in.
Looking at his men for guidance,

As he realized what I told him.
"No, this cannot be true
We have only been with each other for a fortnight.
You would have no clue,
If you carried a baby this night."
"That is where you are wrong, Arthur.
My kind knows as soon as it happens."
I smiled as he looked like he was about to be sick on
his partner,
Until one of the men stepped forwards and gave me a
harsh slap.
"This changes nothing my lord,
It is one of their blood.
Our plan must go forward,
With violence we must flood.
"She must die just like we planned,
For once she is dead the shield with disappear.
We can attack their land,
And make them all naught by a smear.
"We will be rid of this scum,
For once and for all.
We will no longer be forced to slum,
With these cretins across the wall."
"You cannot be serious,
You would kill your own child?
Are you delirious,
Or just that vile?

"I can see your men being heartless and cruel,
But why are you willing to risk the life of your
offspring?
This does not have to be some duel,
But if it is you will deal with my eternal haunting.
I will not let you sleep,
Without you knowing what cruelty you have flung.
You will cry and you will weep,
But what you will do will never be undone."
My words sound ominous,
To even my ears.
But I was just being honest,
As well as picking at Arthur's fears.
But it wasn't enough,
I could see the resolve cloud over his face.
He was so corrupt,
That nothing I said would save my race.
"You will die by my hand."
He stated as he drew his sword.
"I will clear your kind from this land,
Until the balance is restored."
"You can go screw your balance!"
I yelled in his face.
"I hope you choke on your malice,
And I curse you with your fate."
With a single blow,
My life came to its end.

I bled out in a fast flow,
As my soul began to ascend.
Red spattered the ground,
As my body slumped forwards.
I watched my midsection spellbound,
As everything spilled outwards.
It is a terrible feat to die,
But even worse to watch your child so.
She spilled out without a cry,
Striking me a final blow.
He may have killed me,
But worse he killed my child.
I will never allow him to be free,
Of the guilt and pain through which he smiled.

The Watery Grave

Chapter Twenty-Four

'Everyone wishes that the man whom he fears would perish.' -Ovid

I floated over my prone body,
My baby's soul already gone.
My glowing shield with my death became foggy,
And shattered in the oncoming dawn.
It was as though it were made of glass,
And my death became the hammer.
For it shattered in a mass,
Giving way in a sparkling manner.
In a way it was a beautiful sight,
At least until my people were revealed.
Taking away their protection outright,
And revealing our world that was no longer sealed.
The wall of protection was destroyed,
My people no longer safe.
They would be plummeted into the void,
They were doomed to a horrible fate.
I was forced to watch in horror,

As the men ransacked my village.
Destroying them all with torture,
In a vision that was bone chilling.
Screams rang out through the air,
As pools of blood flooded the ground.
The men rained destruction without a care,
Killing all who they found.
True, my people fought back,
Warriors and healers alike.
But this was a surprise attack,
Making it a much harsher strike.
They were gutted before my eyes,
Running the waters in red.
The men, women and children's cries,
Making all feel pity, even the dead.
I floated through the destruction and death,
Until I found what I had been looking for.
My family's screams could have been heard by the deaf,
As they stood on the burning floor.
My mother, my sisters and even my Grand-mama were sentenced to the flames,
Locked within our family home.
Arthur set fire to the frame,
Laughing as it became my family's tomb.
I watched on in a ghostly silence,
As my kind was all slain.

The land was destroyed by violence,
The water ran red with pain.
Their bodies were not given a proper burial,
But a harsh watery grave.
Their chests cut open and stuffed full of rocks from
the area,
And they sunk them deep past the crashing waves.
My family's souls rose to the light,
But my time in this world was not yet up.
I could not leave with those villains still in sight,
They too needed to drink from deaths deep cup.
What I failed to do in life,
Would be my mission in death.
I would keep those on this land alive,
And be their guardian even if I didn't draw breath.
But first I had to take care of a promise,
To send these men to hell's fiery depths.
They would from now on only know darkness,
Until I saw to their deaths.
So I stalked the men for years,
Until a conscience finally grew.
And they caved to their terrible fears,
Losing their lives as was due.
But with my vengeance done,
And my spirit staying,
I had yet to begin,
My soul's aging.

I watched as my once peaceful lake,
Was drained into a valley and river.
But my family's bodies still lay in the wake,
Of the water's fierce quiver.
To me the water no longer held peace,
But rapids of crying souls.
Their bodies long deceased,
But never buried in proper holes.
So I walk the waters,
To calm the rapids,
That grow stronger the longer they harbor,
The bodies thrown in by a savage.

The Woman On The Hill

Chapter Twenty-Five

'I learned that courage was not the absence of fear,
but the triumph over it. The brave man is not he who
does not feel afraid, but he who conquers that fear.' -
Nelson Mandela

This is now my existence,
To be the guardian of these waters.
You heard of my life and my mission,
And know how I was the cause of a slaughter.
I lost the family I loved so dear,
And I lost the child I never knew.
So now I walk these waters here,
In my white, hooded cloak and bare feet too.
I do not punish myself for my actions,
I just try to do better in death.
Because I now know they pain that absence,
Can cause for those who still draw breath.
You wonder why my waters are never peaceful,
But fierce and crashing currents.
It is all because of the psychotic evil,

That took so many lives creating this disturbance.
Most of those bodies are not in peace,
But filled completely with hatred.
The rocks weighed heavily on the souls of the
deceased,
Never being given a grave that is sacred.
So instead they pull others under,
Wanting company in their deep, dark depths.
Hating all who wander,
Into the place of their death.
So now I walk Dunvegan Park,
Guarding both the living and deceased.
Keeping them safe in both the light and the dark,
Doing what I can to make sure their lives do not
cease.
I was not able to help my fellow ghosts,
Before they found their end.
But in death I keep them from becoming engrossed,
In the evil that tries to make their souls descend.
As I walk the waters,
Their spirits finally calm.
No longer wishing to slaughter,
All those who dare to tread on.
I cannot speak for them all,
Because some were evil from the start.
They have done things that appall,
And make it seem as though they have no heart.

But for the other three who have told their tales,
They have nothing to fear.
For their souls hold a goodness that prevails,
Over evil that much is clear.
I am just that whispering voice,
That they sometimes need in their ear.
Steering them to the right choice,
So that the living does not fear.
But my guarding does not end with ghosts,
But involves the living as well.
Doing what I can from my post,
To see that they do not become a shell.
I show my form,
To those who need to see.
So that I can force,
Them onto the path they were meant to be.
The reason my existence was not documented until
the bridge,
Was that people were not around enough before.
They were not by the water enough to see my form
glitch,
In one minute here and then gone once more.
But in 1960 the snow was heavy,
And ice covered the hills.
The men's path that they were on was deadly,
In the cold winter chill.
But when I showed them myself,

Walking silently across the bridge.
Their path was altered to protect,
Their lives so that they would not plummet off the
ridge.
They stopped their truck,
To find my figure but it was in vain.
So once they were on their way with luck,
They went slowly and their steering was contained.
I do not tell this for praise,
Nor do wish for any.
I tell you this so that you understand my days,
Are spent helping many.
I am the woman on the bridge,
But the lady of the lake and river too.
I walk the area like a ghostly witch,
Wishing only for all to travel safely threw.
I was struck down by betrayal,
Because of charisma and a pretty face.
My actions shameful,
And now my existence a lonely disgrace.
So I make it up to my people,
And my daughter as well.
Lending a hand where it is needed,
To keep others from having to dwell.

Death

Epilogue

*'Deep into that darkness peering, long I stood there,
wondering, fearing, doubting, dreaming dreams no
mortal ever dared to dream before.'*
-Edgar Allan Poe

We are the Ghosts of Dunvegan Park,
The ones who met unfortunate deaths.
We use our afterlife to lurk,
On the land where we drew our last breaths.
We are the Woman on the Hill,
Who lost her life to the cold.
Because of a terrible chill,
Her child she could no longer hold.
We are the Nun in the Hills,
Who learned a secret hidden deep.
Who followed on their heels,
But got caught while she did creep.
We are the Priest in the Rectory,
Whose knowledge was his undoing.
He learned of a secret that led to treachery,

Ending with his documents being destroyed from
viewing.
We are the Lady on the River,
Whose heart won out over her head.
Causing her to watch everything she loved wither,
And turn the water red.
We are the lost souls that stayed,
But there are still many others.
With stories that have begun to fade,
And not spoke of like another's.
They are stories hidden deep,
And their spirits are not witnessed.
But just like us their souls weep,
For their deaths that came with a quickness.
Our tales are sad and terrible,
Full of loss and pain.
But we have stayed in a parallel,
Where we will forever remain.
But we are not the only one on this land,
There are others who have stayed.
Some are stuck while others planned,
To stay forever in this glade.
Their tales are all different,
Just as ours were.
But ours are the interest,
That draw the living to our door.
So you know our tales,

But they're not yet done.
We still travel these trails,
In our ghostly fun.
We will rest here for many years yet,
For we will not grow old or die.
Many still have to setting their debt,
With the one who left their souls to cry.

Watch for the next book in this series
They Walk In Darkness
Coming Soon

About The Author

Donna J.A. Olson has always had an (somewhat strange) imaginative mind. From a young age she loved to come up with stories and imagine different characters, and what their lives would be like. Donna has always loved to read and will read anything and everything she can get her hands on. She lives in Northern Alberta with her family and her many animals. When not reading or creating new lives with her writing Donna enjoys riding her ATV, playing with her animals, fixing things, just having fun and enjoying life. She currently has multiple works published through Kobo, Polar Expressions Publishing, The Poetry Institute Of Canada, Hektoen International, Coteau Books and hopes to have more soon.

Facebook: www.facebook.com/donnajaolson
Twitter: @donnajaolson
Instagram: @donnaj.aolson
Website: http://tootsie213dj.wixsite.com/donnajaolson

Lightning Source UK Ltd.
Milton Keynes UK
UKHW020405240720
367054UK00008B/159